MW01138429

This book belongs to
Kimberly Reiprich

JOHN AUDUBON

YOUNG NATURALIST

Written by
Miriam E. Mason

Illustrated by Cathy Morrison

ISBN 1-882859-51-0 (978-1-882859-51-1) hardback
ISBN 1-882859-52-9 (978-1-882859-52-8) paperback

Patria Press, Inc.
PO Box 752
Carmel IN 46082
www.patriapress.com

Printed and bound in the United States of America
10 9 8 7 6 5 4 3 2 1

Text originally published by the Bobbs-Merrill Company, 1943, in the Childhood
of Famous Americans Series®. The Childhood of Famous Americans Series® is a
registered trademark of Simon & Schuster, Inc.

Library of Congress Cataloging-in-Publication Data

Mason, Miriam E. (Miriam Evangeline), 1900-1973.
    John Audubon, young naturalist / by Miriam E. Mason ; illustrated by Cathy
Morrison. -- 2nd ed.
        p. cm. -- (Young patriots series ; v. 12)
    Originally published: John Audubon, boy naturalist. Indianapolis : Bobbs-
Merrill, 1962.
    Summary: As a young boy first in Haiti and then in France, James Audubon
delights in the wonders of nature but on arriving in the United States, he decides
to become an artist and draw every bird in North America.
    ISBN-13: 978-1-882859-51-1 (hardback)
    ISBN-10: 1-882859-51-0 (hardback)
    ISBN-13: 978-1-882859-52-8 (pbk.)
    ISBN-10: 1-882859-52-9 (pbk.)
1. Audubon, John James, 1785-1851--Juvenile fiction. 2. Naturalists--Fiction. 3.
Artists --Fiction. 4. Birds--Fiction. [1. Audubon, John James, 1785-1851--Fiction.] I.
Morrison, Cathy, ill. II. Mason, Miriam E. (Miriam Evangeline), 1900-1973. John
Audubon, boy naturalist. III. Title. IV. Series: Young patriots series ; 12.
    PZ7.M416Joh 2006
    [Fic]--dc22

                                                              2005029406

Edited by Harold Underdown
Design by: TM Design

This book is printed on Glatfelter's 55# Natural recycled paper.

Contents

Illustrations

Chapter 1

The Captain Arrives

Long ago, a little boy opened his brown eyes sleepily and gave a wide yawn as he stretched himself awake.

"Something is different about this morning," the young boy said to himself. He wondered what it was.

Jean was in bed in his own room, the same room in which he had gone to sleep and wakened each evening and each morning for as long as he could remember.

He could see the same mosquito-netting curtains hung about his bed like a veil to keep out the hordes of hungry insects which were always there, ready and waiting to take a bite of nice, tender boy.

The green shutters were closed, as always, to keep out the blazing sunlight of the West Indian island where young Jean lived. A few beams of the bright sunlight managed to creep between the shutters and make slender white lines on the floor.

Some little sugar birds which had come in through

the kitchen door were hopping about the furniture and hunting insects on the floor.

"There is nothing different about you," said the little boy to the sugar birds. They were tame animals which came into the house every day and went quietly about picking up crumbs and bugs and flies.

Outside the house, the trogons and the gorgeously colored chatterers were quarreling in the mango trees, making more noise than usual.

When the boy listened with his sharp ears, he could hear the voices of the laborers down in the cane fields. They were singing in deep, slow, musical tones.

"It is the same song that they always sing," said young Jean. He yawned again and slipped out of bed, looking carefully before he set his slim bare feet down on the floor. In this hot country, a huge tarantula, or poison spider, might come in for a visit. Or a long snake might choose to take a nap in the cool shade of a bedroom.

Jean ran to the window and threw open the green shutter. White sunlight flooded the room with a blast of oven-like heat. Far beyond the mango trees was the sea, so brilliantly blue that it hurt his eyes to look at it. The green cane waved gently in the steep fields which rose from the sea. While he looked, Jean could see what looked like a tiny dark cloud moving above the shoreline, high in the sky.

"The swallows are leaving!" he cried.

Now, suddenly, he knew what had made this morning different. He hadn't heard the morning songs of the blue-gray birds which spent several months of the year in Haiti. Usually, they had wakened him every morning with a shrill, sweet chorus outside his window.

He leaned out still farther, almost falling from the window, in order to watch the dark cloud as it moved swiftly away.

"Goodbye, goodbye, goodbye!" he called, waving his hand. A strange feeling of loneliness came over him, for he loved the swallows.

"Someday I would like to follow the swallows and see where they go," he thought.

Captain Audubon, his father, had told him that the birds went north, many of them to a place called North America.

"When I grow up, I am going to follow those birds to North America!" he said to the birds in the mango trees.

The trogons laughed and laughed, and the chatterers scolded in their harsh voices.

"Silly, silly, silly!" they seemed to say.

Just then Celestine came rushing into the room. "It is time you were up, you sleepyhead!" she called.

She was a tall enslaved woman who took care of the little boy and his sister. Jean's mother had died when he was too young to remember her very well. Since then, Jean's father had put Celestine in charge of the children.

Jean looked surprised. Usually Celestine let him sleep in the mornings.

"Why are you in such a hurry?" asked Jean. He picked up his ruffled shirt from the floor, shaking it well to get rid of any spiders that might be hiding in it.

His old nurse took the shirt from his hand. "Not that one!" Celestine then went to the chest in the corner and got out another shirt. It was a very fancy one, made of finest linen with many little tucks and ruffles.

"But that is my very best shirt!" said Jean, opening his hazel-brown eyes in wide amazement. "Why do you want. . . ."

"The best is none too good for you to wear when the Captain is coming," the old woman interrupted.

The boy's eyes sparkled. He clasped his hands, hardly able to believe this wonderful news. "The Captain—Captain Audubon—my captain?" he cried.

Celestine led him to the window and pointed to the sea. "Look closely," she said.

Yes, there was a ship, resting gracefully like a beautiful white-winged bird on the bright blue water of the sea.

"It is Captain Audubon's ship," whispered Jean happily. Old Celestine nodded her white-turbaned head.

"He came in last night," she said. "His ship arrived late. He came up from the shore and would have wakened you and your sister, but I would not let him." She fastened his shirt. "Hurry now." she said. "We must make you presentable."

In the kitchen his little sister was sitting in her cradle. Her face was very clean, and she had on a brightly colored silk dress trimmed with golden buttons and lots of silver lace.

Jean did not complain when Celestine rubbed his face until it ached. The Captain, his captain, was home from sea!

More than anybody in the world little Jean loved and admired big Jean, the Captain. He thought him the grandest person on earth.

"Ow!" he cried, as old Celestine's comb scraped through his long, light brown curls, yanking out tangles.

The sound of a carriage outside made him forget his pain. The Captain was here!

Captain Audubon came into the kitchen, and Jean jerked away from Celestine and flew into the big man's outstretched arms.

"You are here, Father! You are honestly here at last!

I thought you would never come!" he cried eagerly.

Captain Audubon hugged his son. Then he picked up little Rose and tossed her into the air. He caught her as she came down laughing and screaming with delight.

"Have you really missed me?" the Captain asked, turning back to Jean.

The boy nodded his bright head. "It seems like years—hundreds of them, even thousands!" he answered.

Captain Audubon was of medium height with a friendly face and sharp eyes. Sometimes when he wanted to look dignified, he put on a uniform with many brass buttons and wore a white wig on his head. Today, however, he merely wore the uniform and left his grayish-brown hair uncovered.

He sat down at the table, and old Celestine brought some breakfast—a platter of chicken and some bread and fruit.

"That will do, Celestine," said the Captain. "You had better go. You have many things to do, and I can look after the children."

Celestine went off, her head bobbing angrily. She was muttering to herself.

"She is very angry this morning," said young Jean, biting into a banana. "I slept too long. The swallows did not awaken me, because they left early."

Captain Audubon waited a minute before he spoke. "No, she is angry because, , , " He did not seem to know what to say, and young Jean looked puzzled.

Suddenly the Captain laid down the chicken leg that he had been eating. "Listen, my boy!" he said. "I am taking you away with me—you and your little sister. We are going across the ocean in a ship!"

"In a ship? Across the ocean? As far as—as far as the swallows go?" Jean asked.

The Captain nodded his head. "We are going to France. I have a new mother for you. She is a kind woman, and she is eager to welcome her two little stepchildren!"

"A new mother," whispered Jean. "A French mother! That will be nice." Then his voice grew more eager and his hazel eyes shone. "Shall we see the swallows again?"

Captain Audubon laughed. "I think you are more interested in birds than in a new mother," he said teasingly.

He was pleased, though. He had taught young Jean the names of many birds, and he had told him about the long journeys which the northern birds make to hot countries before the weather grows cold.

"France is a long way off," he said kindly, "but you will find many of your old bird friends there to welcome you. I am sure you will see the swallows, the

"Listen, my boy!" he said. "I am taking you away with
me—you and your little sister. We are going across
the ocean in a ship!"

firebirds, the kingfishers, and the catbirds."

Jean felt happy. He had learned to know these northern birds by sight and song. He had looked forward to their coming in the winter, and he had been sorry when they left the "big heat" of Haiti every year for their cooler northern homes.

"Will there be other birds, too, Father?" he asked eagerly, forgetting to eat his breakfast. "Will there be birds I've never seen—maybe French birds?"

"Oh, dozens of them," laughed the Captain. "You will see the green sandpipers wading in the marsh. You will see jackdaws and crows and owls. You will see the cuckoo, too lazy to build her own nest."

Jean sprang to his feet. He was excited by the thought of all these strange new birds.

"How soon can we start?" he cried. "Can we start right now?"

He was not afraid of the long journey which lay before him, nor of the strange people in that far-off land of France. He was on tiptoe with eagerness to get started on this first flight.

Chapter 2

A New Mother

At times, Jean felt that he had been sailing forever on this great, green tossing ocean. Far behind him, and almost forgotten now, was his old home on the steep mountain island of Haiti.

This was in the year 1789, and swift steamships had not yet been built. Ocean travel still was long and slow.

Every day the little boy asked, "Will we see France today, Father?"

"Not yet, my boy," Captain Audubon would answer kindly.

Often he took young Jean walking with him along the deck of the ship. Hand in hand, father and son walked back and forth, around and around the spotless deck. Jean held his head high and tried not to fall when the ship rolled on the rough waves.

While they walked, the Captain told young Jean exciting true stories about his own life. Captain

Audubon had had many adventures. And there were twenty-one children in his family.

Jean liked to hear his father tell this. "Say it again! Twenty-one children!" He held up the fingers on his slim little hands. "That is two times as many fingers as I have."

"Two times and one over," the Captain said. He was always careful that Jean should count correctly. A boy who cannot count can never become a captain, he told him, because captains have to work many long, hard problems.

"There were twenty-one children in my family," the Captain said again. "When I was twelve, I went to sea as a cabin boy."

No matter how often the Captain and Jean went walking, nor how long they walked, the stories never ran out. The Captain had been in wars, he had been captured and put in a prison, he had even fought with pirates.

"And you always got away!" said young Jean proudly. "I am glad. It would be dreadful to be shut up where you could not get away!"

One day when Jean looked out over the deep green water, he saw a strange bird. At first he thought he must be dreaming, for what would a bird be doing, far out in the ocean?

"Look!" he whispered to Captain Audubon. When

the Captain followed the little boy's finger, his face grew serious.

"That is a stormy petrel," he said. "It loves what men fear—an ocean storm." The petrel was a dark, silent bird a little larger than a parrot. It had strange, three-toed feet, and it seemed to be walking on the water.

"What a sad bird," said young Jean.

"Wait until a storm comes up," his father answered. "When the clouds are darkest and the wind highest, and when the ship is tossing about on the waves, then the petrel dances on the water, laughs, and has a good time."

A few days after this a storm did come up. The masts of the ship shook in the wind. The cables and chains cracked and groaned. The storm was so fierce that little Rose cried. Even the sailors were frightened.

Jean was not frightened. "Let me go with you, Father," he begged. "I am not afraid to be on deck in the storm. I want to see the petrel dancing and laughing on the waves!"

At last the Captain carried the little boy in his arms up to the dark, wave-swept deck. Jean looked out at the foaming waves. Yes, there it was. The stormy petrel was riding the wild waves, and it seemed to be laughing.

"You are not afraid of the storm, and I am not

Jean saw several birds on his long ocean voyage.

afraid of the storm," thought Jean. "I am a stormy petrel, too."

Jean saw several birds on his long ocean voyage. He saw the greedy white pelican which eats as much as six men. He saw the black cormorant, with its stiff, fan-shaped tail.

When at last the merchant ship approached the

13

shore of France, Jean saw a great loon, green-black in the sunlight, spread its wide wings and dive for a fish.

He was so thrilled that he did not even hear the joyous cries of the sailors, "Land ho!"

"See, Father, he got the fish! He got it!"

"Indeed he did. He seldom fails," replied the Captain gently. Then he lifted the boy high in his arms.

"See, boy! There ahead of us is France. We are nearly home!"

Jean strained his eyes to the dark line of land which lay ahead. He looked back over the endless miles of green ocean water. He wondered if the little swallows had crossed these wide waters safely and were waiting to greet him in his new home.

"So many houses!" gasped Jean, looking about him with wonder.

At last the little group of travelers had come to the town toward which they had been journeying for so long. This was the city of Nantes, in France, on the Loire River. It was one of the oldest and richest towns in France with many narrow, winding streets, tall houses crowding close to one another, and the cathedral tower rising high above the rooftops.

Captain Audubon came down the gangplank of the ship with young Jean holding tightly to his hand, and Celestine carrying Rose.

Jean had forgotten all about the weariness of his long journey. He was aglow with excitement over this strange new town.

The Audubons and Celestine climbed into a carriage, the coachman closed the doors, and the carriage rumbled down the streets over the round cobblestones.

"There is the river Loire," pointed the Captain as they rattled along. Jean looked at the river. "And there is the great cathedral," his father continued.

"Look, Father, look!" whispered Jean excitedly. "Stop the carriage, please!"

"I never knew you to be so interested in cathedrals," said the Captain, in a pleased voice.

But Jean was pointing down to the river. There among the wiry grasses stood a strange, long-legged bird.

"That bird, Father! See how it stands on one foot there among the grasses. Please let me out. Let me go down and look at the bird!"

Captain Audubon was a little irritated. "No need to be in such a frenzy, my boy!" he said. "That is only a sandpiper. The Loire is thick with them. They will wait."

On and on through the winding, narrow street rumbled the Audubons' carriage. At last it came to a stop before a tall, dignified house in the very heart of Nantes.

"What a high house," said Jean, bending his head back to look up to the steep roof of the French house. In Haiti all the houses had very low roofs.

He looked about him with interest as they went up the steps and into the house. In Haiti there were grass mattings on the floor and shutters to keep out the blazing white sunlight. Here the carpet was quite soft with beautifully colored flowers woven in it.

Soon a smiling lady came into the room. Her silk dress made a whispering sound when she walked, and there was a sweet smell about her, like flowers.

"This is your new mother, children," said the Captain, and the lady smiled again. Jean knew he would love her.

"What a handsome boy he is," she cried, "and what a beautiful little girl!" She hugged Jean and whispered into his ear, "Do you like candy?"

When he nodded his head she said, "We will get a new suit for you. There will be big pockets in it. There will be plenty of room in the pockets for coins and candy!"

"Will you let me go down to the river and catch one of those birds? Will you let me have it for my own?" He told her about the bird which stood on one leg.

"Certainly!" laughed his new mother. "How bright

he is," she said to Captain Audubon. "Not many boys his age would be interested in the sandpipers."

Then she added, "I have a bird, too. Come, I will show you!"

She led him to the dining room. Out there a green parrot was sitting in a big cage. A monkey was playing on top of a cupboard.

"The parrot's name is Migonne," said his new mother. "The monkey is Giorgio. They can be your pets, if you like."

"I am glad we came here," said Jean happily.

He had a parrot to remind him of his old home back in Haiti. He had a monkey to play with. He had a kind new *maman* to love him.

Outside, below the cobblestone streets of this funny-looking French town, was a river where strange, beautiful birds stood on one leg or dug in the mud with their bills. Jean felt very happy about everything.

Jean was dreaming. He thought he was back in Haiti in his bed with the mosquito-netting curtains around it. Celestine had turned into a big trogon with an extra-large bill. She was sitting in the mango tree outside his window, calling and calling him to get up.

"Go away, Celestine," he said crossly. "I want to hear the swallows singing."

Then he remembered that the swallows were gone from Haiti. They had gone a long time ago. He had watched them go and wished that he could follow them.

Suddenly he opened his eyes.

"It is not a dream. I do hear the swallows!" he thought. He looked about him. He was in his bed in the new home. The windows were wide open, and the soft wind was blowing through the room. The light was a soft gold.

Again he heard the singing. He jumped out of bed and ran to the window. Out there was the world of rooftops, chimney pots, and high steeples. Below his window was a little garden with an elm tree spreading its graceful branches to the ground.

And there, close up under the eaves of the house, were the swallows! They, too, had made the long journey across the ocean. They had come here before him, and already they were busy building their mud nests under the eaves.

Now Jean felt that he was really at home. This strange house, in a city crowded with close-together houses, suddenly seemed very familiar to him, for here were old friends that he already knew and loved.

The cool sea air made him feel wide awake and strong. He could think of a dozen things to do today. He was glad that the swallows had wakened him so early.

Chapter 3

Jean Makes a Trade

Jean felt very rich this morning. In the pocket of his trousers was a whole handful of great big brown coins. He rattled them as he ran down the two flights of stairs from his bedroom. They made a cheerful sound.

Time had passed quickly since he and his little sister had come to Nantes. Now they felt as if they had always lived in the tall, quiet house in the heart of the city. They could not imagine what it would be like to be without a kind, smiling stepmother like Maman Anne.

The morning was very beautiful. It was April again, and the weeping-willow twigs were covered with tiny golden buds. Thrushes were singing in the elm trees. The garden was filled with violets and primroses and flaming yellow daffodils.

He planned to run down to the candy store and spend some of the coins which his stepmother had given him.

As he came downstairs he heard loud, heartbroken wails coming from the back court. "Good gracious!" he said to himself. "Why is Rose crying like that?"

He hurried through the parlor with its rich, brightly flowered carpets and high-backed chairs, and on through the narrow hall to the sunny kitchen.

Out there little Rose was howling at the top of her lungs. Big tears were rolling down her cheeks. The cook was petting her and trying to comfort her, but Rose could not be comforted.

"What in the world. . . ," Jean began. Then he looked to where the cook was pointing. On the floor lay poor little Migonne, dead. Giorgio, the monkey, watched gravely from the high cupboard to which he had scrambled.

"That wicked, wicked monkey has killed Migonne!" sobbed Rose. "Migonne did no harm. She only reached for a bit of food."

"It was Giorgio's breakfast," said the cook kindly. "Giorgio wanted it for himself."

Now tears ran down Jean's cheeks, too. The parrot was such a beautiful creature. He knew he would miss her. Without her steady screaming, the house would seem very solemn.

"That evil monkey must be punished!" he said. Then he went over and picked up the parrot and stroked her feathers tenderly.

"That wicked, wicked monkey has killed Migonne!"

"If we could put some sawdust and cotton in Migonne like that in your doll," he said to his sister, "we could keep her with us for ever and ever."

"No, no, no!" cried Rose. "I want a funeral for dear Migonne. I want candles for her and flowers and much sadness. I want a grave for her under the weeping willow tree!"

Jean looked stubborn. "Then we would never see her again, Rose," he argued. "We have to stuff her and keep her with us!"

Rose cried harder and harder. Giorgio, from his place of safety on the cupboard, began to imitate the little girl. He chattered and scolded loudly.

Jean had to shout to make his voice heard. "Migonne is mine. I am going to keep her!"

The cook put both hands to her ears. Just then, Madame Audubon came running into the kitchen to see what had happened.

"Wicked, wicked Giorgio!" she cried when Jean explained what the monkey had done. "You will be chained after this! You will not be allowed to run free."

"I want a funeral for Migonne!" sobbed Rose pitifully.

"I want to stuff Migonne so that she will be with us forever!" cried Jean.

Their stepmother thought for a moment. She was a

wise, kind woman, and she wanted to be fair to both children. "There are two wishes and only one parrot," she said. "One of you must give in to the other."

Jean felt in his pocket. The coins rattled and reminded him that he had started to the store. He took out the money and put it on the kitchen table.

"Look, Rose," he said. "You may have all my money. You can buy candy with it, or you can go to the market and buy another pet. A rabbit doesn't cost much. You will still have money left for candy."

Rose wiped her eyes. "I will name the rabbit Migonne," she said sadly. The quarrel was over. The cook washed the tears from Rose's face. Madame Audubon called the monkey down, and Jean carried Migonne away to his father's room.

"Father will tell me what to do next," the young boy said.

Chapter 4

Birds of a Feather

Jean spent countless hours watching the brown and white thrushes in the shade of the weeping willow trees. They were dainty, beautiful birds with reddish-brown feathers. Their throats and breasts were white, and there were tiny heart-shaped spots of dark brown on the white feathers. Often, as he lay quietly under the willow trees watching the birds, he had been close enough to see the markings on their feathers.

Sometimes he had taken his pencils and paper with him and tried to draw pictures of the birds as they ate their meals or walked about. Whenever he moved, however, they flew away. He could not get close enough to draw them.

One day he went to market with the cook. There he got an idea. Thrushes were often used for food in France. They are plump and tender and make lovely pies. On market days there were always thrushes for sale, just as there were chickens and geese and ducks.

"I will buy some for myself," he decided. He counted all the money he had. It was enough for five birds.

"Five birds of my own!" Jean exclaimed. He hurried home to his room and laid them in a row on his bed. Now he could really look at them and see the different colors in their feathers—red brown, olive brown, white. And the white eye rings which made the bird look as if it were wearing spectacles—now he could get close enough to see the tiny, tiny white feathers which made the rings.

Somehow, though, the dead thrushes didn't look like birds any more. They just looked like rag dolls or bunches of brown feathers.

Jean sighed. He reached into the drawer of his writing desk and got the pencils which his father had given him. He chose one that had just the right shade of rich, reddish brown. He tried to draw a picture, for a picture was a way of keeping something forever.

"I won't draw my birds lying on their sides like feather dusters on a shelf," he thought. "I want my birds to look alive!"

He closed his eyes for a minute and remembered how he had once watched two thrushes eating their breakfast of beetles. He had been so close to them that he had held his breath while he watched, so that he would not frighten the shy little things away. They had eaten the wriggling beetles quite daintily. Thrushes

"I want my birds to look alive!"

had beautiful table manners, he thought. They were as graceful and elegant as a prince and princess.

They were not like the gluttonous pelicans that gobbled down a fish at one gulp. Nor were they like the humble little sugar birds. Birds behaved as differently as people did.

So he worked and worked all morning, but ended up with nothing but five lifeless bunches of feathers on his bed, and many queer-looking smudges on his paper.

At last a loud knock and his father's voice aroused him from his efforts.

"Jean, my boy!"

"Yes, Father?" he answered.

"What are you doing? It is long past noon and your mother is worried you are lost."

Jean unlocked his door, and the Captain came in. He gave a quick, surprised look at the row of birds on the bed, and at the floor, strewn with sheets of paper.

"Have you been robbing the cook's pot?"

"Oh, Father, I wanted to make the birds my very own by drawing them. But I cannot make them seem real in my pictures."

Jean's cheeks flushed, and there were tears in his eyes.

The Captain patted his shoulder. "There, there, my boy," he said. "You are not the first artist who has tried to catch a bird with his pencil and failed."

Then he took the little boy's hand and led him out of the room. "Come and eat. You will feel better when you have some food."

They sat down to a belated meal in the dining room, but Jean was too sad to eat.

"I was so sure I could draw them, Father," he said, "if I could only get close enough. But the dead thrushes were so horrible."

He pointed to a picture which was hanging above

the mantel. It was a picture which was very stylish for dining rooms in those days—a painting of three dead fish on a platter.

Jean shuddered. "My birds were like those fish, Father, only worse."

Just then a song sounded through the open window. "Uoli-a-e-o-li-noli-noi-aeolee-lee!" came the long, flute-like notes.

Jean ran on tiptoe to the window. "There it is! There is my thrush the way I wanted it to be!" he whispered excitedly. Among the leaves of the lilac bush was a spotted thrush, singing with all its heart.

"Birds were meant to be free!" he thought. "I must learn to make my birds like that—free, alive, moving!"

Early the next morning, Jean hopped out of bed and into his clothes. "Today," he said excitedly, "I shall spend the day drawing."

Suddenly, he remembered that his stepmother had other plans for him. "Oh, well," he thought, "tomorrow will be soon enough."

Jean spent the morning in his room. After the noon meal, he dressed for the events of the afternoon.

"You are the handsomest boy in France," his stepmother said fondly when she saw Jean. She gave him a kiss on each cheek.

Then she pushed him back gently so that she could look at him more closely. He really did look very handsome. His light brown hair had been brushed till it shone like silk, and it hung in waves to his shoulders. He had on a lovely new green coat which had just been brought by the tailor, a new suit, new shoes with silver buckles, and a shirt of the softest linen, all tucked and ruffled.

"I can hardly wait for my friends to see you!" cried Madame Audubon. Today she was having a party in her drawing room, and had invited many of the finest ladies in Nantes.

Downstairs everything was ready. The servants had dusted the elegant furniture until it shone like polished metal. Great jars of blossoms stood here and there in the rooms.

In the kitchen the cook had been very busy, preparing the delicious little pies and cakes which the guests would eat.

Musicians had been hired to come and entertain the company. The finest string quartet in Bretagne would play the lively tunes of the day—the minuet, the pavane, the gavotte—and other dainty French music.

"But you, you are the real treasure which I shall enjoy showing off," said his stepmother, kissing his cheeks again. "All my friends will envy me when they see that I have such a handsome, witty, clever son!"

"How you spoil the lad!" said Captain Audubon,

coming into the room. But he smiled. Jean did not seem to be hurt by his stepmother's gushing. He was as generous, as friendly, as happy as any boy could be. Of course, he was not very good at his mathematics, but the Captain hoped he would get better as he grew older.

It was still a little while before time for the guests to arrive, and Madame Audubon had to dress Jean's little sister and herself.

"You are ready, and you may walk about for a while in the garden," said Madame Audubon to Jean. She added anxiously, "Do not sit on the garden seats. They may be dusty."

Jean went outside and walked carefully about in the garden. He was glad his stepmother was pleased with his looks, for he loved her very dearly. He was careful not to sit on the garden seats, and he resisted the urge to climb the trees.

"If I keep walking, I will not mind having to stand up," he thought. He went out the garden gate and thought he would walk down toward the river, not very far, but far enough to take up a few more minutes of time.

He soon breathed in the damp smell of the river, and he saw the wide Loire with its banks edged with the tough green salt grasses.

"I will be very careful not to get close enough to

muddy my shoes," he thought, looking at the silver-buckled slippers on his feet.

Suddenly the young boy saw something that made his heart leap and filled him with a strange excitement.

There, walking gracefully among the tough grasses in the damp river ground, went three green sandpipers. They were tripping lightly along, singing in clear, piping voices.

"Ah!" whispered Jean. The green sandpipers often came here, because it was so near the ocean. These were beautiful sandpipers—the biggest and greenest that Jean had ever seen.

"If I could only draw them and keep them forever, just as they are!" thought the boy. "I wish I had brought my pencils."

He walked behind the long-legged birds, going very quietly so as not to startle them. His new shoes sank into the soft, marshy river bank, but he hardly noticed that.

"Perhaps if I hide in the grass and watch them for a long time, I can remember them well enough to draw them!" he thought.

The sandpipers had long legs like stilts, and long, sharp bills. They were hunting for food in the marshy bank of the river, digging for worms, insect eggs, or tiny shellfish. The biggest sandpiper raised its bill with a crawfish wriggling in it.

"I must remember how he holds his head up and how the claws of the crawfish wave in the air," thought Jean. He sank down on his knees in the marshy grass. Mud oozed over his legs and above his knees, but he hardly noticed it.

The birds went on eating, piping softly to each other in their soft, musical tones and not bothered by the boy's bright eager eyes which followed every movement He watched the birds bore into the mud, feel around with their bills, and raise their heads with food.

"They feel with their bills, just as I do with my fingers!" he thought. He was learning something by watching these birds.

So he lay there in the harsh salt grass of the Loire, watchful and fascinated, while the afternoon passed by.

At last one of the birds raised its head and looked straight into the boy's eyes. Quick as a wink, then, it raised itself into the air on its long pointed wings. The others followed. As they rose, Jean could see their white breasts and greenish-black feathers.

Then he stood up. He was covered with mud from head to toe, and he was wet and chilly. In his hand he held a long, greenish plume which had dropped slowly to the ground as the sandpipers flew toward the ocean.

"It must be nearly time for the party," he thought in sudden dismay. "I must hurry!"

He ran swiftly up the street toward the house, and neat ladies looked after him, frowning as he passed them, and muttering things about "dirty ragamuffins."

He dashed breathlessly into the beautiful drawing room of the house. "Is it time for the party?" he asked.

Elegantly dressed ladies were just getting ready to leave. They stared in astonishment at the mud-covered little boy who stood on the flowered velvet carpet with a long green feather in his hand.

Little Rose, dainty as a rose in her pale batiste, pointed reproachfully at Jean. "Shame on you, you dirty boy!" she scolded. "The party is nearly over, and here you come looking worse than a street beggar!"

The ladies tried not to laugh as they looked at the boy. Could this be the handsome young stepson about whom Madame Audubon had been bragging? It did not seem likely.

"I have been to the river," Jean said to no one in particular. "I saw three green sandpipers. One of them had a crawfish in its bill. One of them looked at me. . . ."

"And flew away in fright at what it saw, no doubt," said a pert girl in brocade.

Madame Audubon put her silken arm about

. . . neat ladies looked after him, frowning as he passed them . . .

Jean and drew him closer to her.

"You see!" she cried proudly. "My son has brought me a handsome quill for my writing table. He knew I had been wanting one. Is he not the most loving son in France?"

Wheatstacks

"Oh, Jean, you are so excited!" said his little sister crossly. "You chatter like a parrot! You fly about like a setting hen! I've never seen you in such a frenzy!"

"You are the setting hen!" said Jean indignantly, looking at his young sister as she sat quietly on her ladder-backed chair in the hall. Her hair was brushed and curled. Her white muslin was spotless. Her little feet in their black slippers were primly crossed in front of her, and her tiny clean hands rested in her lap in a ladylike way.

But Jean kept rushing up and down the stairs to see if he had forgotten anything. He had his pencils and crayons and paper. He had the book of bird pictures which his father had given him last Christmas. He even had the two stuffed thrushes, which he had nearly forgotten. He couldn't leave them behind.

The family was getting ready to leave their

town house to spend the summer in the country, at Wheatstacks.

Jean could hardly wait. He stood at the window, impatiently watching for the carriage to rattle up the cobbled streets. At last it came.

"I thought you would never get here!" Jean called angrily to the coachman. He remembered his manners enough, however, to hold the door open for Madame Audubon and his sister. He waited for them to rustle down the steps and climb into the carriage.

Then, with his two stuffed thrushes in his hand, he jumped down two steps at a time and climbed up by the coachman. Captain Audubon would join them later, when he returned from a sea voyage.

The whip cracked, and they were off, rattling down the streets of old Nantes, and around corners where jackdaws peeked at them from their dark hiding places in walls and roofs.

"Goodbye, you thieves!" called Jean happily, waving at them.

Swallows sang in the courtyards of the old houses and swept about in their strange, swift flight. Jean looked at their shining blue-gray wings and forked tails. "How could such small pinions have carried the birds so far?" he wondered. "It doesn't seem possible."

On the carriage rolled until it reached the end of the cobbled streets and came to the country road.

Black ravens and carrion crows fluttered up from the fields like a cloud of smoke. Black and white magpies hopped over the soil, chattering in their rough, cheerful voices. The carriage drove on, past a heavy stone church with a tall spire about which the swallows fluttered.

Then at last the Audubons came to the village of Couëron, nine miles from Nantes. Couëron was a sleepy, dusty little farm village, and in the midsummer sunlight it looked unusually drowsy.

"Please go very slowly past the old windmill," Jean begged the driver as they came to an old mill with a tall tower.

This very old mill near the farm was called the Tower Mill, because it had a high tower built on it. Once the Tower Mill had been the biggest and busiest in the town of Saint Nazaire, but now it was tumbledown and empty. The miller had died long ago, and people of the village said the tower had been haunted since his death.

"I want to see if I can see the ghost in the tower," said Jean. "I have heard the villagers say that it looks out of the top window and says, 'Hoo-hoo!' at people."

But nothing looked out of the tower window as the carriage passed by, and no ghostly voice said, "Hoo-hoo!"

"The ghost is asleep this morning, as it ought to

"I want to see if I can see the ghost in the tower," said Jean.

be," said the driver. He winked at Jean. "All good ghosts sleep in the daytime."

"Some day this summer I am going to climb into the old tower and look at the ghost," planned Jean. "I will see what a ghost looks like in its sleep."

Jean was now ten years old, and not afraid of ghosts that lived in old mill towers and said, "Hoo-hoo!" at people.

Soon they were out of the village and passing old farmhouses, built of rough gray stone and covered with moss and vines. Great ricks of straw stood in the fields, and birds busily hunting dropped grain filled the brown stubble of summer.

Now the family came in sight of Wheatstacks— which in French was called La Gerbetière—a tall, handsome house of cream-colored limestone. To Jean, this country place of his father's looked like a mansion with its swelled, slated roof, tall cupola, and balcony.

The house was built on a hill which overlooked the river and the wheatfields which gave it its name of Wheatstacks. From the very top of the hill, one could see Nantes, nine miles away.

Into the house went the family, glad of the cool shade after the long ride in the sun. Maman Anne opened windows and looked for dust and mildew. Rose ran upstairs to her room to see if the dolls which she had left asleep last fall were still sleeping.

Jean dumped his possessions in a heap on his floor and carefully put the two stuffed thrushes on the bed. Then he looked to see if his treasures from last year were safe. He found his glass box of birds' eggs, the tortoise shell, and his mud swallows' nest—all just as he had left them. The snake skin, for which he had traded his silver shoe buckles last summer, had not fared so well. It had been badly eaten by mice.

"Perhaps I can find another one, a real green viper," he thought, looking at the ruined snake skin with regret.

He could look through the window and see the orange trees with the blackbirds singing in them, and beyond the orangery was the barnyard, with geese waddling about. Still farther he saw the grassy, flowery riverbank, shaded with walnut trees. Jean knew white and yellow water lilies would be floating on the water, and that blue dragonflies would be hovering above the flowers.

And farther down, where the ocean tide met the river and the red fishing boats lay drowsily in the sunlight, he might see stilt birds. Stilt birds were funny creatures, no bigger than pigeons, which stood on bright red legs 15 inches high. He knew he would find long-billed curlews hunting for beetles and hidden treasures in the mud of the river bank.

"Jean, please come and find a ripe orange for me!"

called his sister. But Jean was already gone, running through the orangery and down to the meadow where the redshanks and curlews were waiting for him and the river was coaxing him to join in their treasure hunt.

"We are in time for the blessing of the fields this year," Maman Anne said later.

The blessing of the fields and orchards was a beautiful ceremony which was held each year by the priests and the people of the village. It was always held very early in the morning between dawn and sunrise. Usually it took place in the early springtime, but this spring the priest had been sick and unable to go out.

Now he was well again, and even though it was early summer, the people of Saint Nazaire still wished to have their fields and orchards blessed by the priest.

"May we all walk in the procession, Maman?" asked Jean eagerly.

Little Rose added, "May I wear my best white dress with the blue ribbons, Maman?"

"Yes, of course, children," Maman Anne answered gently.

Jean was awake next morning when the servant came to call him, though it was very early. Out in the yard the early birds were just stirring, making sleepy little sounds as the pale light of dawn came into their nests.

Down in the kitchen Maman Anne, Jean, and Rose quickly ate crisp croissants and drank hot chocolate. Then they started out for the village church.

The light was blue and shadowy at this hour before sunrise. Dew lay on the grass like a silver veil. Jean liked the feel of the cool dampness against his bare legs.

More people joined Madame Audubon and the children as they came out into the road. By the time they reached the church at the edge of Couëron, it looked as if everybody was going to join in the procession.

Soon Father Jacques and a visiting priest came out of the church. They looked very handsome and dignified in dark robes and white linen surplices. They held great jugs of holy water in their hands.

The two priests walked ahead, and in a double line behind them came all the people. The priests sang a very solemn hymn as they walked. The words to the hymn were in Latin, and Jean did not understand them.

The priests and the long double line of people walked through the rich farm lands, past shining brooks, past great fields of late violets, along narrow green paths, and across brown plowed fields.

They went through the orchards, and the birds

joined in the song. Then the children sang a little song to the birds.

The priests scattered holy water from their jugs and called out a blessing.

"Bless the earth and all its produce!

"Bless the wheat, the wine, the fruit, and the flowers.

"Bless the water we drink, and the grass we tread on!"

The sun rose higher. It warmed the morning breeze and made a happy light on the faces of the people. The birds sang louder.

Last of all the priests blessed the people, and the ceremony was over for another year.

"It will be a good year," said an old lady to Madame Audubon. "Did you see how many swallows were here? Swallows bring good luck!"

Chapter 6

A Scarecrow Meets
a Ghost

Jean was lying out under the cherry trees in the orchard. The cherries were getting ripe, and the blackbirds were greedily feasting on the juicy fruit.

The cook had sent Jean to the orchard to throw stones at the blackbirds and drive them out of the trees. But Jean was not interested in throwing stones at the blackbirds. He was only interested in watching them.

The birds were very black, but he noticed how their feathers changed when the sun shone on them. Then they seemed suddenly to turn to fiery colors—violet, blue, copper, and green. Their eyes were round and yellow. Now and then one stared down at the quiet boy, as if wondering what sort of a scarecrow he was.

"Ouch!" cried Jean, putting his hands over his ears. "You sound like a whole field of rusty wheelbarrows!"

He knew blackbirds could not sing very well, but

this did not seem to bother them. They tried just the same. Their voices sounded wheezy and cracked, like broken whistles. When such a large chorus of them sang at once, the noise was almost deafening.

Soon the carriage rolled up from the barn, and his stepmother and sister came out of the house and got in. They were dressed in beautiful muslin dresses and were carrying their best parasols.

"Don't let the blackbirds fly away with your nose, Jean!" called Rose, waving her hand at him. She had grown into a very dainty, ladylike little girl, and sometimes she was a little ashamed of her brother's looks.

Jean was happy when he saw the carriage disappear. His father was away. Now his mother and sister were away, and nobody was around to ask him where he was going.

Dear Maman would have been sure to say, "But, darling, what if you should fall from that great old tower!"

His little sister might even have cried, for she always wanted to hurry fast by the old windmill tower.

"I am not afraid of any ghost that cries, 'Hoo-hoo' at children," thought Jean bravely. "I would just like to see a ghost! I'd draw a picture of it!"

With no more thought for the blackbirds, he raced

out of the orchard and down the lane toward the old mill tower.

He didn't stop and look for birds' nests along the way, or see if he could find another tortoise to add to his collection. Today he was going to meet the ghost.

Behind him in the cherry orchard the blackbirds fluttered and ate and gabbled in their rusty voices. They were very happy to have the cherry trees to themselves. Jean was the kind of scarecrow they liked.

"I'm not a bit afraid," said Jean to himself, as he came to the old windmill. He didn't believe in ghosts any more than he did in witches or fairies.

Still, his heart was pounding fast and hard as he came to the lonely old mill. He put his hand over it and felt the quick *beat, beat, beat.*

"Like the heart of that little field hare which we caught in the meadow last week!" he teased himself. Then he took a long breath and held his head high.

"I am the son of Captain Jean Audubon," he said. "He is one of the bravest men in the world and has fought pirates, sailors, and soldiers. I am the son of a brave man!"

He looked all around him, but there was no one in sight, not even a farmer in the field. Only a busy chickadee, industriously hunting for cankerworm moths and their eggs, stopped pecking for an instant and stared at the boy in a friendly, curious way.

Jean listened. He wondered if the ghost was looking at him from the ramshackle tower. He did not hear any sound from the mill. Only the silvery tinkling notes of the hard-working little chickadee and the sad musical call of a cuckoo in the field broke the summer stillness.

He pushed open the door and jumped as a frightful screech sounded on his ears. Then he laughed. It was only the rusty hinges of the old door, screaming for oil. He stepped inside.

The light in the mill was very dim. Old, old dust from a forgotten grinding lay about the floor. Mice scurried swiftly away on their tiny feet. Bits of corncobs and chaff lay about.

"Nothing here!" said the boy cheerily. His voice sounded quite strange to him.

A crooked stairway led upstairs. He went slowly up the steps, looking about as he went. Long black cobwebs were draped like ghostly veils along the stairway, and a plump spider, swinging back and forth on a long silver thread, almost landed on his inquisitive nose.

"I have seen many bigger spiders than you!" said Jean. But his voice was quite soft. Somehow, a loud voice sounded out of place in this silent, ghostly, dusty mill.

There was nothing more dangerous upstairs, either. "Nothing here but dust and cobwebs," he reassured himself.

His heart was beating very fast. There was a ladder leading up to the tower. It was an old tumbledown ladder and it led to a dark little trap door, far above him.

He went up the ladder. Some of the rungs were missing. He almost fell when one broke under his foot. He went slower as he came near the top.

At last he put his head through. "Hello!" he said. There was no answer. "Hello there, Mr. Ghost!" he said in a louder voice. Still nothing answered. He stepped into the old tower.

He looked around. There was no ghost up here. There were only more dust and cobwebs and scampering mice.

Suddenly a board broke beneath his foot. He caught at something to keep from falling. It moved under his hand. A wailing, groaning noise came to his ears, and the clanking sound of a chain. But before he was really scared, Jean saw that he had caught hold of the old chain which turned the mill wheel. It had made the noise.

He looked around. There was still no ghost. But he felt out of breath, and he sat down for a minute to rest.

Then he heard it. Had the villagers been right? There was the Noise, very plain and very close. "Hoo-hoo!"

Jean looked all around. He did not see a thing and that made it worse. "Maybe I had better be going!" he thought. After all, the cook had told him to keep the blackbirds away from the cherries, and he did like cherry pie.

He turned around quickly. And there, almost at his nose, he saw the strangest creature. It was hiding in the darkness of the tower eaves, and it looked at him silently.

"A cat!" whispered Jean. It had big yellow eyes, pointed ears, and an unfriendly face. But its nose was not at all like the nose of old Fifi, the kitchen cat. Its nose was—yes, it was long and hooked!

"And it has feathers!" thought the boy, very puzzled, as he stood back and gazed. The feathers were brown and yellowish. They were very much like Fifi's fur, but they were feathers all the same.

"I wonder how many feet you have?" thought Jean, burning with curiosity. He put out a hand to touch the creature.

It hissed at him fiercely and struck his hand. A long red scratch spread across the top of his hand. Jean hardly noticed the stinging pain.

"You hiss like a cat. You stare like a cat. You have

"I've seen a cat with feathers."

ears like a cat and feathers like a bird, and your beak is like a parrot's beak. Are you a cat or a bird?"

The creature hissed again, and then it suddenly unfolded a pair of wings and flew into another corner. Jean continued to watch. Then he saw the weird thing catch a mouse—exactly like a cat would.

"You are too much for me!" cried the boy. He scrambled quickly down the rickety ladder, down the crooked stairway, and out through the creaking door.

He had seen the ghost, but what was it? "What a strange creature!" Jean exclaimed. "I've seen a cat with feathers."

Chapter 7

An Owl and an Egg

As he came near the house, Jean saw something which made him feel excited and delighted. A carriage was just pulling up in front of the Audubon country place.

"Could it be Father?" Jean wondered, as he watched a figure step from the carriage. Then he saw that it was his father. He would have known that stocky figure in the old sea jacket a mile away.

He ran faster, forgetting the heat and the dust, and nearly knocked the Captain down with his joyful hug.

"I have brought you a present I know you will like," said the Captain later on. He took a big square box from among the many trunks and boxes he had brought with him.

"Open it now. I want to see what you will say," insisted the Captain. Jean cut the rope and lifted the lid of the box. He looked. Then he stared.

"It is. . . it is the ghost!" he whispered.

It had the same staring yellow eyes. It had the brown and yellowish feathers, so like a cat's fur. And it had the cruel, curved nose like a parrot's beak.

The Captain laughed and laughed. "Ghost, indeed," he said. "That is an owl, my boy—a genuine owl from the faraway land of North America!"

Jean touched the owl with a careful finger, and the Captain laughed again. "He will not hurt you, my boy," he said. "He is a stuffed owl, and he came from the finest taxidermist in Philadelphia!"

Jean lifted the bird out and looked at it. It really looked almost alive. Its yellow glass eyes looked just like the ghost's eyes. Its two feet were clutching a piece of wood.

"It is beautiful, Father, beautiful!" he cried. "I want to make a picture of it."

He thought a minute.

"I wouldn't draw my owl looking straight ahead like this, holding a piece of wood between its claws. I would draw my owl in the dark corner of an old barn holding a mouse in its bill—a live mouse, Father!"

Again Jean paused for a minute. Then he said, "If I hadn't already made plans for tomorrow, I would see if I could find my owl."

Captain Audubon smiled at his son. "I hope you have included your lessons in your plans. They must come first."

"In the country," thought Jean, waking up early, "I don't need an hourglass—I can tell time by the birds!"

At the very crack of dawn, and long before sunrise, the swallows began to chirp in their sweet, shrill voices. Jean knew he would not need to get up yet, but could turn over and sleep some more.

Then the pigeons joined in the song. Wheeling out from their attic home in the barn they cooed and chanted. Jean began to think about all his plans for that day and to wonder what the weather had in store for him.

A few minutes later the blackbirds began their song in the cherry trees, and he sat up in bed and yawned to make himself wide awake.

When the finches added their low, sweet, happy notes to the chorus, he got up and dressed.

There was only one shadow on the golden sunshine of these summer days in the country, and that was the shadow of lessons. Some lessons were not so bad, but lessons in mathematics were awful. And, sad to say, the Captain thought that mathematics was the most important thing that Jean needed to learn.

"Without mathematics you can never be a captain," he said sternly. "You cannot even be a rear gunner— without mathematics!"

The midsummer morning was sweet. Jean listened to the swallows, to the pigeons, and to the blackbirds. Suddenly he had an idea. He would get up with the blackbirds this morning and not wait for the finches. Blackbird time was very early—the Captain would not yet be up.

Jean slipped softly into his clothes and started down the stairway. He crept past his father's door, as silently as a field mouse.

Ah! He had made it! He was outside the house and free—free as a bird!

A skylark sprang into the air singing, and the boy watched it until it disappeared into the sky. He felt thrilled. For a moment he felt as if he were in the tiny body of the bird, rising against the wind, singing to the morning sun!

This morning he wanted to find some hedge sparrow's eggs to put with his collection. He walked slowly along the hedgerow, looking among the thick green leaves for the little bluish-white eggs that would be hidden carefully away from the field mice and snakes.

Soon he heard the mellow "K-k-k-k-kowkow-ow-kow" of the cuckoo. He sank softly down in the grass to watch, for he had learned that he could see many wonderful things if he only sat and watched.

When he had sat very quietly for several minutes,

looking this way and that, he saw the cuckoo sitting on the ground in the grass. Neither the boy nor the bird moved. He noticed the red circles about the bird's eyes, its black bill, and the grayish white throat. He wished for his crayons.

After many minutes the bird rose into the air, chanting its mellow, clucking song. "The cuckoo is looking for something, too," thought the boy. He kept still.

He crouched low, watching. He had heard that the careless cuckoo never builds a nest, but lays its eggs in the nests of other birds to be hatched. Now he was going to see.

The brownish, pigeon-shaped bird flew straight to the hedge. The boy held his breath in anticipation. In a minute or so the cuckoo came out again and flew gaily off, chanting its "K-k-k-k-kowkow-ow-kow!"

Jean ran swiftly to the hedge and pushed aside the leaves. What he saw delighted him. There, carefully built in the heart of the bush, was a little hedge sparrow's nest. He bent low. He saw five tiny bluish white eggs with rusty spots on them. And right in the center of the sparrow's eggs he saw another egg—a bigger one, of a different color—the greenish egg of the cuckoo that did not build her own nest.

Very carefully Jean lifted the pale green egg from the sparrow's nest.

"A treasure I have been wanting for a long time!"

In his pocket was a great sack of candy, and in his hand,
tenderly held, was the cuckoo's egg.

he thought happily. No gold-hunter would have been more excited or overjoyed than he was to possess the cuckoo egg.

Jean was surprised to see how high the sun had risen. And suddenly he realized that he was hungry. He was hungry and quite a long way from home, and breakfast would be long over in the kitchen of Wheatstacks.

This did not worry Jean. The village of Couëron was almost in sight, and there were two candy stores and a bakery in Couëron. He had no money, but that did not matter. He knew that his stepmother had arranged for him to buy all the candy and cakes he wanted on credit.

Soon, humming happily, he came back down the road. In his pocket was a great sack of candy, and in his hand, tenderly held, was the cuckoo's egg.

"See, Maman!" he cried, as he arrived home. His stepmother and his father were sitting on the breezy balcony which overlooked the river. "See what I have found!"

The Captain looked sternly at Jean.

"You have been to the village," he said. "You have been to the village when you should have been home studying your mathematics!"

Madame Audubon put her arms around Jean and kissed him on each cheek.

"He went on an errand for me, Captain!" she said. "He knew my sweet tooth was aching and aching for some aniseed bonbons! Is he not the dearest and kindest son in all France!"

"And you," whispered Jean into her ear, "are the sweetest *maman* in all the world!"

Chapter 8

From Nature
to Lessons

Autumn transformed the green and brown coun-
tryside, and it turned yellow and copper and gold,
blood-red and purple.

The farmers brought in the corn, piled high on the
wagons. They dug deep holes in the ground for pota-
toes and beets and cabbages. The holes were lined
with straw and had little funnels of straw sticking
above the ground.

The farmers brought the cattle in from the green
river islands where many of them had been browsing
all summer.

Delicious golden pears and misty purple grapes
were ripening against the wall. Ripe apples lay on the
ground in heaps like jewels—red ones, yellow ones,
russet brown ones.

It was time for the Audubons to say goodbye to the
country and go back to Nantes.

The great cream-colored house would be locked

up for the winter, and all the family had things to do. Madame Audubon wiped and polished each bit of silver and china before she locked it behind the cupboard doors. She aired the linens and made sure that everything was clean.

Rose kissed her dolls good-by and tucked them away in their beds.

Jean wished he could take all his treasures to town with him, but there was no room in his little bedroom.

So he took a last look at the cuckoo's egg, the stuffed thrushes, the dried snake skins, the feathers and tortoise shells and wasps' nests which he had gathered that summer.

He hated to leave the corn crake. He was very proud of it, for he had stuffed the bird himself, and it looked almost alive. Its long legs were clasped about a beech twig, and it held a grain of corn in its bill.

"I wish I could take you with me," he whispered, smoothing the feathers of the corn crake. Then he added, "But you will be here next summer when I return!"

"Come, son!" called his father. Jean gave the bird one last look and ran out the door, closing it behind him.

The October air was crisp today. Rose was wrapped in her crimson cape with the hood that came over her curls. Madame Audubon was wearing a quilted jacket.

"My beloved boy, you will be cold!" his stepmother

cried as Jean came out. "Where is your good russet cloak?"

"I do not know, Maman," answered Jean truthfully. The russet cloak had been new last spring. It had looked rich and beautiful when the tailor brought it home.

"Surely you brought the cloak," puzzled Madame Audubon. "Yes, I remember well. You wore it to church, and how handsome you looked! Do you not remember?"

"Yes, Maman," answered Jean, "but it is gone now. It is not in my wardrobe. I am certain it is not there!"

He did not tell his stepmother what had happened to the cloak. He could not bring himself to confess to her that he had traded it to a farmer boy for the corn crake which was up in his bedroom. He knew this would make her unhappy.

"I've grown too tall and big for a cloak," he had thought. "But I'll never grow so big or so old that I won't be thrilled by the sight of that long-legged corn crake, holding tight to the beech limb and reaching out to bite off a grain of golden October corn!"

"You are the handsomest boy in all France," Maman Anne told him. "You must have the education of a gentleman."

There were no free public schools in France then. Private teachers were hired by those parents who could afford them.

Jean had several teachers, because he took many kinds of lessons. He had music teachers who taught him to sing and to play the violin, the guitar, the lute, and the flageolet.

The flageolet, a small instrument something like a flute, was Jean's favorite. Jean had learned that he could imitate the songs of birds on the flageolet.

He had spent many hours during the summer just listening to the birds' songs and memorizing their melodies. He had come to the conclusion that bird musicians have favorite places for their music, just as human musicians do. The birds' songs sounded best at the edge of a woods or beside a stream or in a garden.

Jean liked his music lessons, and he would practice for a long time on the stiff, dainty little French tunes which the master gave him.

When he was alone, however, he liked to pick up the flageolet and play the lovely songs of his feathered masters at Wheatstacks. When he imitated the soft notes of the mourning dove, or the sweet pure whistle of the chickadee, or the fast, whispering song of the woodpecker, the walls of the house and the crowded roofs of Nantes seemed to drop away. He would be back in the country again with the fields and woods about him.

His dancing teacher reminded him of the country too. He was a small, elegant gentleman who wore a fashionable white satin vest under his long-tailed black suit.

"He needs only a pair of wings to make him look exactly like the pied wagtail," Jean often thought, as he watched the dancing teacher doing the steps of the gavotte or the minuet.

"One, two, three, swing, bow!" the teacher would say to his pupils.

There had been many wagtails in the damp meadows about Wheatstacks. Jean had often watched them as they half walked, half ran along the ground, swinging their tails as they moved. They were very clean, prim little birds, too, Jean had noticed, always bathing and washing in the shallow water.

"Are you listening, Monsieur Audubon?" the dancing teacher said sharply. "Bow to your partner!"

Jean pulled himself back from his dreams. He bowed quickly—so quickly that he bumped his partner's head.

"Yes, indeed, pardon me, Monsieur Wagtail!" he said politely. He could not understand why the other children laughed, the teacher looked angry, and his sister blushed with shame.

He could not understand why the other children
laughed, the teacher looked angry, and his sister
blushed with shame.

Chapter 9

A Gift for a Lady

Jean came home from a walk one day to find his sister very much excited.

"Guess what!" she cried. "We have received an invitation to a party, a wonderful party!"

Jean held his basket behind his back so that Rose would not notice the water which was dripping from the family of frogs he intended to keep in his room.

"Is that any reason why I should go into a frenzy?" he asked. "Parties are not unusual."

"This party is special," insisted Rose. "It is a birthday party and a dance. There will be musicians from Paris. But that is not all!"

Jean moved his basket from one hand to the other. Cold, muddy water was slowly dripping down the back of his legs to the flowered parlor carpet. In a minute Rose would be sure to notice it and cry out in horror.

"I may not be able to go to a party in two weeks," he said. "There is a sandpiper's nest down by the river.

I watch it every day. I would not miss the hatching for a silly party."

Rose opened her eyes wide and told the most exciting part of her news.

"This party is for Cecile d'Orbigny," she said. "It is her twelfth birthday!"

"Well!" said Jean. He moved the basket again. "That is different. Perhaps I had better go then!"

Cecile d'Orbigny was almost the prettiest girl in Nantes. She went to Jean's dancing class, and she usually chose him as her partner in the ladies' choice. And Jean always chose her except when the dancing master frowned at him and said, "You must not always bow to the same lady, Master Audubon!"

So now Cecile was going to have a party of her own, and there would be musicians from Paris to play for the dances!

"A birthday party will call for a birthday gift," he commented.

"Maman has said I may select my own gift for Cecile," Rose said happily. "I may go to all the shops and select the gift I think is most beautiful. One that is not too expensive, of course," she added.

"I shall not worry about the cost," said Jean carelessly, picking up his basket of frogs, and starting up to his own room. "Maman will give me as much money as I need."

"She is more likely to give you a good thrashing when she sees the mud puddle you have left on her carpet!" called Rose.

Jean hardly heard this threat. Already his quick mind was at work on the question of what to get Cecile for a birthday present.

It must be something very, very special. It must be beautiful. It must be rare. Cecile was such a pretty girl. She had many curls, the color of the wheat fields at Wheatstacks in midsummer. Her cheeks were very pink and her lips were very red, and she smiled often. She was graceful, too—almost as graceful as a bird. Monsieur Wagtail never had to scold her for awkwardness.

"This is a very important problem," thought Jean. "I must give it some thought!"

The very next day Jean started out to search for Cecile's gift. With his pockets full of big copper coins, he walked briskly down to the street of shops.

"Something for a young lady, please," he said when the shopkeeper came up bowing and smiling. He added, "Something very fine. It is for a birthday gift."

The shopkeeper showed him many nice gifts. He showed him a music box which played three different tunes.

"She has a spinet. She can play many tunes for

herself," said Jean, shaking his head.

The shopkeeper got out a golden mirror with a design of flowers and angels on the back.

"The very thing for a beautiful young lady," he said. Again Jean shook his head.

"My sister is going to buy her a silver mirror. I want something different."

"I have the very thing," whispered the man. He brought out a beautiful carved box. It had many strange little articles in it. There were bits of black plaster, tiny boxes of paint and powder, and some little brushes.

"This is what all the court ladies use to make themselves beautiful," he explained. "Here is the beautiful pink for the cheeks, the red for the lips, the black for the eyelashes."

"The lady is too young to wear so much paint on her face," said Jean.

"I have the very thing!" cried the patient shopkeeper again. He went to the back of the store and returned with a long box. Inside was a lovely wax doll with cheeks as pink as Cecile's own, and a real wig.

"The lady is too old for dolls," said Jean.

The shopkeeper showed him a golden snuff box, a silver cup, and a brooch with many jewels in it. But Jean thought none of these things were good enough for Cecile.

Inside was a lovely wax doll with cheeks as pink
as Cecile's own, and a real wig.

"I will come back another day," said Jean at last,
and the shopkeeper sighed.

Jean walked home slowly, trying to think. He
walked through a meadow, down by the river. There
the green reeds grew tall and slender. Hidden among
them was the sandpiper's nest with the eggs which he
had been watching so carefully.

Suddenly the boy saw something new and exciting. Curled around the silvery stalk of a cattail was a slender little green snake. It was watching something, too. It was watching a dragonfly which was flitting lazily through the air just above the snake's head.

"Beautiful!" whispered Jean. The silvery cattail, the pale green of the snake about it, the eyes like the jet beads on Maman's dress, the rainbow gauze of the dragonfly's wings—all these things fascinated the boy.

Suddenly the little snake snapped swiftly at the dragonfly and swallowed it. Then, its feast over, the small creature uncurled gracefully and glided away in the grasses.

Jean went shopping the next day, too, but he went to a different shop this time. "A gift for a lady, please," he said again.

The polite shopkeeper got out necklaces, bracelets, rings, and glittering shoe buckles.

None of these seemed quite right, nor did the silver platters, the glass wine bottles, nor the handsome carving sets which the shopkeeper paraded for Jean.

Suddenly on a high shelf behind the shop keeper he saw something. It was a tall, silver candlestick. It looked something like the cattail stem on which the little snake had curled.

"I will take the silver candlestick, please," he told the shopkeeper.

He was glad that he had ten days left before the birthday party. He had solved his problem, but still had to find the rest of the gift. The next thing was to get a small green snake and have it stuffed so that it would look perfectly natural.

"Have you decided on a gift for Cecile?" asked Rose, that evening, and Jean nodded with a happy, mysterious look.

His gift would be the finest one at the party!

Finally the long-awaited day arrived.

"It will be such a lovely party!" chattered Rose. "I do hope Cecile will like my silver mirror! Don't you think my flowered muslin dress is beautiful, Jean?"

She whirled about on the toes of her little satin slippers, and her ruffled dress stood out like a parasol. Jean thought she looked very pretty, almost exactly like a wax doll. He was proud of her, but of course he did not wish her to know it. She was already far too vain.

"At least you look better than the scarecrows at Wheatstacks," he admitted. Jean himself was looking quite handsome in a fine new silk shirt, trousers with knee buckles of silver, and shiny new shoes.

"Please tell me what you have for Cecile's present," teased Rose, but Jean chased her out of the room.

"It is a surprise—a beautiful, exciting surprise!" he called. "I want Cecile to be the first to see it. I know she will be pleased!"

After Jean was sure that his sister was no longer around, he took another look at his precious gift. He was so proud of it that he could hardly breathe. He was counting the minutes till Cecile should see it.

"She will clap her hands! She will cry out in delight! It will be her favorite present!" he thought again.

Jean's present for Cecile was the slim silver candlestick which he had found in the jeweler's shop. But that was not all. Wound about the candlestick, so carefully that it looked almost alive, was a little green snake.

"One who did not know would never dream that you are only stuffed, my little pet," Jean said to the creature. He had even put a dragonfly in the snake's mouth.

Of course, the snake had rather a strange smell, but that would go away after a while. It was not unusual for stuffed creatures to smell rather queer at first.

Jean had traded a pocketful of coins, another pocketful of sweets, and one of his shirts to the boy who had killed the snake for him. He had given a silver coin to the taxidermist for stuffing the snake.

"Later, perhaps, I can give her a much bigger

snake and stuff it myself," he thought. "I must practice first, though. Only a neatly stuffed snake is good
enough for Cecile."

At last the coach came, and the two children were
soon rattling over the cobbled streets toward the tall
house on King's Boulevard where the d'Orbignys lived.

"Does it seem to you that there is a very odd smell
in the carriage?" whispered Rose to Jean. "I am going
to tell Maman that Pierre must be more careful about
keeping it clean."

Jean did not answer. He was dreaming of the
moment when Cecile would unwrap her present, and
of the delight on her face when she looked at it.

The d'Orbigny house was very festive-looking with
carriages crowding the street in front of it. Jean and
Rose went up the steps with other dressed-up young
ladies and gentlemen.

"Be very careful with this package," said Jean, as he
handed his gift to one of the servants. He could hardly
wait for Cecile to open his present. He wished that
opening gifts was the first thing instead of the last.

Cecile was standing in the hallway to greet her
guests. She looked beautiful. Her party dress was
made of shining silk trimmed with many ruffles. She
wore a garland of colorful roses in her hair.

"Happy birthday, Cecile," said Jean. "You look as
pretty as a parrot!"

When the musicians from Paris began to play the minuet, Jean bowed before Cecile.

"Will you be my partner?" he said. Then he added in a whisper, "I have a beautiful, beautiful, surprise for you!"

Cecile tried to guess. "Tell me only what color it is," she begged.

"Part of it is green and part is silver and part is rainbow colored," Jean answered.

Cecile's blue eyes became wide and bright. "I can guess," she said. She was thinking of a lovely string of crystal and emerald beads on a silver string which she had seen in the window of the jewelry shop.

Jean looked proud. "No matter what you guess, you will be surprised!" he said happily.

At last the time came for opening the presents.

Servants brought the great pile of gifts into the room and laid them on a table before Cecile.

One by one Cecile opened her presents. There was a tiny music box which played two tunes. There was Rose's silver mirror. There were two bottles of perfume, a white prayer book, and a necklace of dainty pearls.

Jean stood close to Cecile. "I can hardly wait till you see my present," he whispered. "Please hurry and open it."

"I am saving the best till the last," Cecile whis-

pered back. She thought again of the silver and emerald necklace. "How beautiful it will look," she said to herself.

At last only Jean's gift was left. Cecile picked it up. Yes, it was long and slim, just the shape of a necklace case.

The next minute she gave a terrible scream. She dropped
Jean's present and jumped on a sofa.

The next minute she gave a terrible scream. She
dropped Jean's present and jumped on a sofa. She
began to cry at the top of her lungs. She did not look
like a young lady at her first party. She looked like a

little girl, very angry and very frightened.

"Go home!" Cecile shouted. "Take your nasty, horrible, ugly old snake with you. Never come back to my house again!"

The other girls screamed, too, and the boys laughed. They thought Jean had played a good joke on Cecile.

"Stupid! Ignoramus! Pig!" screamed Cecile. "How dare you? I will tell my father and mother! A beautiful gift, indeed!"

Rose's cheeks were red. Her eyes filled with tears. She did not know whether to be angry at Cecile or ashamed of her brother.

After his surprise, Jean shrugged his shoulders. He picked up the candlestick with the little snake and wrapped it up again.

"You are like a parrot in more ways than one! Goodbye, I have had a lovely time," he said to Cecile and bowed gracefully.

"How silly girls are!" he thought as he went out on the street and started to walk home. "They do not know how to appreciate the really fine things of life— not at all!" At first he felt disappointed because Cecile had not liked his present. But he never stayed downhearted for a long time. Soon he began to whistle. By the time he reached home he was quite happy.

Up in his own room he set the candlestick on the mantle. It looked beautiful. If one did not look too closely, it looked like a live snake coiled around a silvery stalk. Now he was glad that Cecile had not liked his gift. A beautiful stuffed snake was wasted on such a silly girl.

Chapter 10

What Will Jean Do?

"They are nothing but a family of cripples!" cried Jean, almost in tears. "They are stiff and dead and ugly, and their tails look glued on and ready to fall off!"

He was looking at the pictures which he had made during the past year. Some people might have thought them good for a young boy, but they did not satisfy Jean.

"They do not look quite right, but give yourself time, my boy," said Captain Audubon, who was in the room with his son. Then he added hopefully, "You do very well indeed with the claws. See how the sharp toes of that blackbird are buried in the green corn blade. They are as natural as life!"

Jean nodded. Feet were easy for him, but tails were very hard. No matter how hard he tried, he was never satisfied with the tails.

A little while later his sister came out to the back

court, sniffing in distaste. "What in the world are you burning, Jean, that makes such a disagreeable smell?"

"I am burning up a family of cripples," answered Jean sadly, stirring the bit of charred paper which was all that remained of a whole year's drawings.

"Tomorrow I will begin all over," he went on. "I will work hard on their tails. I will get them right, Sister. They will be mine forever!"

Rose sighed, shook her head, and walked away. Jean stayed to watch the last picture curl into a bit of black ember.

The next day was a much happier one for Jean. In fact, it was a day which stood out in his life like a great torch.

A visitor from North America came to call on the Audubons.

Captain Audubon owned many properties. Besides the plantation in Haiti, the house in Nantes, and the farm near Saint Nazaire, he also owned a substantial piece of land in North America.

Jean was out in the courtyard, busy with his fencing lesson, when the servant called him that morning.

"The Captain wishes to see you in the drawing room!" the servant announced. Jean laid down the slim blade of shining steel with which he had been practicing, and ran into the house. In the library was a stranger who did not look like a Frenchman.

"This is Mr. Dacosta. He comes from North America. I thought you would like to hear something about that wild, faraway country."

Mr. Dacosta smiled and began telling about the riches of the land, the great farms, the vast forests covering miles and miles of ground.

"Are there birds in those forests?" Jean asked eagerly.

"Uncounted millions of birds, my boy—birds of the most splendid plumage and graceful flight. They gather in multitudes. There are birds called passenger pigeons which cover the whole sky, like a blanket of smoke!"

Before the wide eyes of the boy, he opened a trunk. He took from it an enormous feather.

"This is the feather of the American eagle, or the bird of Washington, as it is often called."

Jean held the great feather in his hands. He closed his eyes and tried to imagine the bird which would have feathers like this. His heart beat madly.

"You would love the parakeets," the man went on. "They are bright and cheerful. The woods are full of them in some places. I have brought one to show you." He took out a stuffed bird. It was bright green, with a red and yellow head and a hooked beak.

Jean remembered something he had almost forgotten—white sunshine on blinding blue water, a fringe of green cane in which laborers stooped and cut, a ghostly veil of mosquito netting fluttering about his bed, and outside, in the mango trees, the brilliant parrots of Haiti.

"Father, I want to go to North America!" he cried, and Mr. Dacosta smiled.

"It is a good land for young men," he said. "It is a land of power and riches."

Jean shook his head. "I do not want the power and I do not want the riches. I want the birds. I want to see them and follow them and touch them. I want to put them down on paper and make them live for always!"

Had he said all this before? He had completely forgotten the promise he had made to the chattering trogons and parrots on that long-past morning in Haiti.

But he knew that more than anything in the world, he wanted to see and to draw the birds of this strange, far-off North America.

Jean turned fourteen in 1799. He was a tall, slender boy with light brown hair and sparkling brown eyes. His radiant smile had not changed very much from the smile that had first won the heart of his beloved stepmother. His father worried that he was not learning what he needed to become a captain or engineer. And so one day, his father took him on a long journey to the town of Rochefort.

It was a rather grim-looking town, built on the side of a rocky hill. Jean had often heard of Rochefort. It was a military town with a naval school. The Captain had a house in the officers' section.

They entered this house. It was very different from the crowded picture-book rooms back in Nantes, or the luxurious country house at Couëron. This was a man's place, bare and stern. Two ship models on the mantel were the only decoration in the room.

"Sit down, my boy," said the Captain, pointing to one of the stiff chairs. When Jean had obeyed, his father said, "My beloved boy, you are now safe. I have brought you here that I may be able to pay constant attention to your studies. Here you shall have enough time for pleasures, but the remainder must be employed with industry and care!"

"Yes, Father," said Jean good-naturedly.

The Captain went on, "This day is entirely yours. As I must attend to my duties, you may go with me if you wish and see the docks, the fine ships of war, and the other sights."

"Yes, Father," said the boy again.

Here he saw no green sandpipers or red-legged stilt birds or curlews hunting food by the water. Here he saw only the tall men-of-war crowding the dock, and officers and sailors and young military students.

"Head up, chin out, stomach in!" roared the young officer, Gabriel Dupuy Gaudeau. He hit Jean a fierce blow between the shoulders to make him straighten up.

"Right, left, right, left," he ordered. The young students were on parade.

Captain Audubon had gone away on another trip, but he had enrolled his son in the military school before he left.

Jean did not like the military school. It seemed to him that the young officer was always finding fault with him.

To Jean, time dragged by horribly here in the Rochefort school. When spring began to come, Jean felt he could bear it no longer. "Now I know how birds feel when they are shut up in cages," he thought, staring out the window of his bare room into the garden of the Marine Secretary.

Suddenly his heart leaped. Was that a swallow out in the garden—a swallow here in this grim place of ships, docks, and soldiers?

Yes, it was a swallow! He had listened too many times to be mistaken. The swallow was back from the south, and it was calling him.

A terrible homesickness came over him. He could close his eyes and see the marshy fields of Nantes with the long-legged beach birds wading about. He could hear the thrushes in the orange trees. He could feel the remembered sunshine of the Couëron meadows.

Outside his door in the hall, Dupuy Gaudeau kept guard. But there were other ways of getting out.

Jean slipped from the window, landed on the ground, and headed for the Marine Secretary's garden.

"Halt!" A young corporal stopped him suddenly. "You are running away! You will be reported for this, Jean Jacques Audubon! There is a grave punishment for such behavior!"

Jean never forgot the miserable days he spent aboard a prison ship, waiting for his father to return. He never forgot the look on his father's face when the Captain came after him, and he never forgot the stern words of the Captain.

He did not try to run away any more. He finished his year of training and came home, looking quite smart in his military uniform. But he never went back to Rochefort.

Jean slipped from the window, landed on the ground, and headed for the Marine Secretary's garden.

Back at Couëron, Jean was able to spend all his time and thought making the pictures he loved. He was learning to use paints and water colors, too, so that his pictures now looked more alive.

He was no longer bothered by the hated mathematics lessons. Captain Audubon had decided that his son was not cut out to be a naval officer or an engineer.

Always, when his father came home, Jean showed him the best of the pictures. The Captain looked at them carefully, now and then giving a few words of kind advice.

One day the Captain called Jean into his study. There was a thoughtful look on his face, and the boy's heart beat faster. Was he going to be sent back to Rochefort, that place he hated?

"Have you thought any more about your future, my boy?" asked the Captain kindly. "You are past sixteen now. I believe it is time you chose your life work."

"I have chosen it, Father," answered Jean quickly. "I want to be an artist and draw pictures of birds."

The Captain sighed. This was not what he had wanted for his only son. But he was wise enough to know that fathers cannot always plan what their children should do.

"Very well, then," he said. "If you wish to choose painting for your life work, you must have a good teacher. We must make arrangements for you to go to Paris."

"To Paris!" Jean cried. Paris was the capital and the most exciting city in France.

"Jacques Louis David has his studio there. He will take you as a pupil."

So young Audubon set forth on a journey, to try to capture the desire of his heart. His hopes were high. Monsieur David was one of the most famous and gifted French artists.

"Perhaps he will teach me to paint in oils, and how to show the blue-green shine of a purple grackle's throat and the shimmer of August sun on green corn!"

Jean was disappointed, however.

"Certainly not, young sir," returned the artist to his question. "You are not ready for oils. You must go into the beginner's class and study drawing from a plaster cast."

"I want to draw animals and birds," cried Jean despairingly when he looked about at his models. They were great plaster casts of giant eyes and noses, and of ancient statues.

He wrote to Captain Audubon. "I do not want to draw great statues and long-dead giants, dear Father. I am afraid that Paris is not for me. I would rather spend my time in the woods and fields with birds for my companions."

Captain Audubon read these words as he sat in his study at Couëron. He had been reading his letters and looking over his accounts.

And then he raised his head. Was it only his imagination, or did he really hear Jean's voice down in the drawing room?

In the next minute there was a quick rush of footsteps up the stairs—for Jean never walked up stairways. There was a rapid knock at the door, and in a minute the stout sea captain's breath was nearly squeezed out of him in Jean's eager hug.

"Jean, why are you home now? Is there a holiday? Is Monsieur David ill?"

"Oh, I have left Monsieur David's studio, Father. Those monstrous eyes and noses and dead statues gave me nightmares!"

Jean laughed. He did not look like a person who was bothered with nightmares. His eyes sparkled, and his long curly hair shone like silk. He was tall and slender and glowing with good health and happiness.

"It is good to see you again, my boy," said the Captain. "But what are you planning to do now that you have left Monsieur David?"

"First of all, I am going to take a long walk in the

fields," Jean answered. "I am sure I can catch a green viper, and I may even find some turtle's eggs to add to my collection."

He put his arm through his father's. "Come with me," he coaxed. "Forget these musty accounts and dreary letters. Maman will have a picnic basket packed for us. We will spend the day together in the fields."

Captain Audubon had always found it hard to say no to his son, and before long the two of them were walking together along the hedgerows of Couëron. They carried a well-packed basket of food between them.

Suddenly Jean stood still, listening and looking. From a hedge came the cries of birds. Jean pointed. "See those wrens? They are a father and a mother, and they seem to be worried about something!"

Quick and silent as a cat, he darted to the hedge. The little parent wrens flew off, scolding and crying. Jean parted the leaves and looked.

In a minute he beckoned to the Captain. He was smiling broadly.

"The poor little wrens do not know what to do," he said, as the Captain came near. "They have hatched a cuckoo in their nest!"

There in the middle of the tiny wren's nest, between the two wren babies, was a much larger bird, which had just hatched. The halves of its broken shell were still in the nest, and it was howling for food already.

"No wonder the poor little wrens are puzzled," laughed Jean. "This queer bird doesn't seem like one of theirs. They don't know how to treat him!"

The Captain looked at the little wren parents, chattering in worried voices a few feet away.

Jean was looking happy and excited. "It is not often that you can find where the cuckoos have put their eggs," he said. "They are sly about hiding them. What wonderful luck to find one after it has hatched! I shall come down here every day and watch what happens!"

The Captain sighed. He felt he could sympathize with those bird parents, fluttering and puzzling over their strange child. Sometimes it seemed to him that he and Mrs. Audubon had a cuckoo in their own nest.

Chapter 11

Bird of Passage

Everyone in the Audubon household was excited. Jean was going away again. This time he was taking a long, long trip, across the Atlantic Ocean to North America.

Maman and Rose had helped to pack his trunks. They had put in many fine clothes—lovely white linen shirts with tucks and ruffles, fine cloaks, good woolen breeches, and shoes with silver buckles.

"The handsomest boy in France must look like a gentleman when he goes to that wild country!" said Maman Anne, wiping tears from her eyes. The Captain had written a letter which Jean was to give to the Captain's business manager in Philadelphia, a man named Miers Fisher. "This letter will be handed to you by my son," he had written. "I hope you will find him a good place where he will learn English and make sound commercial connections."

He also gave Jean a letter to a bank in New York, so

that the boy might get as much money as he needed.

Jean did not forget his violin, his flageolet, his fencing sword, or his gun. He carefully packed his crayons, water colors, and pencils.

Maman Anne wept to see him go. She had heard many tales about the deep woods of North America, and she was afraid for her darling son.

Jean comforted her. "Do not forget that I am one of the best shots in France," he said proudly. "Remember, also, Maman, how good I am at fencing with the sword!"

Rose kissed him goodbye and whispered in his ear, "I know many pretty girls in Madame Duprée's school who will spoil their eyes crying when you leave, my brother!"

"How silly you talk!" said Jean crossly. "Just like a magpie—chatter, chatter, chatter. You know I'm not interested in girls!"

He hated to say goodbye to his room. It had become a real treasure trove through all these happy years.

"I wish I could take you with me," he whispered. "Then everything would be perfect!"

All across the room hung a festoon of birds' eggs which he had gathered carefully, summer after summer. The insides had been blown out and the shells strung to make a chain which the boy thought was far lovelier than any string of jewels could ever be. Across the chimney piece marched his parade of stuffed animals. He had worked long and hard learning to stuff them so that they looked natural. There were squirrels, rabbits, a little red fox, and even a parrot.

He smiled at the parrot. "Rose can have her funeral for you, after all!" he said.

Of course, some people might not like the smell of the room. Rose was always turning up her nose and saying, "Awful!" But it was a sweet, pleasant smell to Jean.

The mahogany shelves which Maman Anne had given him for his books were filled with frogs, fish, turtles, and snakes. Jean gazed at the green baby snake which he had coiled around a silver candlestick and given to Cecile d'Orbigny. She had screamed, but he was proud of it. It looked too life-like to be stuffed.

"I am glad to get away from girls!" thought Jean. He wondered if there was room in his trunk for his favorite green viper.

Then he remembered that Mr. Dacosta had said there were many snakes in the woods of North America. "The forest is alive with snakes and birds," were Mr. Dacosta's words.

At the dock Captain Audubon shook Jean's hand. "I expect great things of you, my boy!" he said. "North America is a wonderful land. You will find riches and perhaps even fame!"

"I shall not give up until I find what I want," promised Jean. "I'll make you proud of me!"

"Farewell, my son," said the Captain sadly. "I had thought you might stay in France and be one of the victorious eagles of Napoleon's army, but perhaps it is better for you to follow the eagles of North America."

The bell began to ring. It was time to go. Jean ran eagerly up the gangplank. At last he was off—off to a wonderful new country where birds flew in millions!

Jean had a good time on the way to the United States. Everybody liked the lively young French boy who could dance so well and make such sweet music with the guitar or flageolet, the violin or flute. The long weeks of the voyage passed more quickly for them all because he was along.

Then came a thrilling morning, when winging out to the ship came a great flock of birds.

"Gulls!" cried Jean. "We are nearing land!"

"Those gulls are from Sandy Hook," Captain John Smith told him in French. "In a short time now, you will see North America!"

"North America!" repeated Jean. The words had a magic sound to him. The gulls swooped low, screaming in their harsh voices, and Jean waved his handkerchief at them.

The gulls swooped low, screaming in their harsh voices...

"They have come out to meet me," he said to the Captain. "They must know that I love birds more than any other creatures on earth!"

"More likely they know that a sailing vessel will always provide them with plenty of tasty garbage to eat," said the Captain. But his eyes were friendly, and he smiled as he gave the boy a hearty slap on the back.

"Here's hoping that the United States will give you everything you seek for, lad," he said. "Remember I'm always your friend. If you need help in a strange country, let me know. A note to Fraunces Tavern will find me."

"Thank you, sir," replied Jean, his eager eyes straining for the North American shore line. He was not at all afraid of the new country. Even the fact that he would have to learn a new language did not frighten him. He had already picked up a few English words from the Americans on the ship. He was glad, though, that the Captain could speak French a little. Few of the passengers knew any French at all.

As it turned out, Jean needed Captain Smith's help sooner than he expected. At that time there was an epidemic of fever in New York, an illness called "yellow fever."

A pathetic letter brought Skipper Smith hurrying to see his young friend. He found Jean sick in bed, feeling miserable and neglected in his hotel room.

"I am afraid my flight has come to a sorry end," moaned Jean.

"Nonsense!" comforted the Skipper in his halting French. "You need some nursing and mothering, and I know the very place for you. Just outside Philadelphia is an excellent boarding-house kept by two kind Quaker ladies. They will soon have you playing the fiddle and dancing again!"

Although Jean did not feel that he would ever want to fiddle and dance again, he found that Skipper Smith was right. The two kindhearted Quaker ladies took good care of him and soon brought him back to health.

They gave him his first real lessons in the English language. He began to call himself John James Audubon, and no longer Jean Jacques. At first it was very difficult for him to pronounce English words— even his own name—clearly.

He was sitting by the window one day when a carriage came to a stop in front of the boardinghouse. A stout middle-aged man in the gray cloak and big hat of a Quaker gentleman hurried up to the door.

"I am Miers Fisher," he said. "I have just learned that the son of my client, Captain Audubon, is here. I have come to take him to my villa near Philadelphia."

Soon the young patient was being assisted into a comfortable carriage. A pretty girl in a gray bonnet and frock was sitting there.

Miers Fisher introduced her as his daughter Sarah. John was glad to see someone near his own age.

"Do you like the music?" he asked in his careful English, as the carriage rolled past gray-stone farmhouses and pleasant fields.

She shook her head. "My father does not approve of music of any kind," she said primly.

John thought of his beloved musical instruments, and sighed. After a minute he asked, "Do you like the dance?"

This time the curls beneath the gray bonnet fairly quivered.

"Oh, no, indeed! My father thinks that dancing is sinful!"

John stared in surprise. His sister Rose loved dancing and music, and so did all the girls in France. "I suppose you sing a great deal?" he tried again.

"Why, no, not a great deal. Only once in a while in church," she answered. She added, "My father does not approve of careless singing."

John felt discouraged. He thought he would not have much fun at Mr. Fisher's house. Before long, however, his spirits rose again. He saw fields, hills, woods, and a river around the Fisher place. He would spend most of his time outdoors with the birds.

Alas, he soon found that Squire Fisher also did not approve of hunting birds, or fishing, or wandering out in the fields. He told his young visitor sternly that he was wasting time, and that such amusements could not be permitted while John was under his charge.

"Then I will not be any longer!" cried John excitedly, as well as he could in his clumsy English. "To be here is like being the bird in the cage!"

"Where could you find a better or more comfortable place?" asked Mr. Fisher.

"I will go to my father's farm at Mill Grove on the Perkiomen Rivière!" declared John. "Do not argue with me, Monsieur Fisher. Here I am the starling in the cage!"

The next morning the carriage came to the door. John and his luggage were stowed away. The whip cracked, and the horses trotted down the Trenton Road toward Mill Grove. Once more the bird of passage was on his way.

John took a long breath of freedom. He took his flageolet from his pocket and began to play. Then he sang.

"On the topmost branch
The sweet nightingale was singing.
Sing, nightingale, sing on,
Joy from your glad heart bringing!"

His own heart was just as happy as the nightingale's heart.

Chapter 12

Mill Grove and Lucy

"This is heaven!" cried John that spring morning when he first went out to explore his father's big country estate.

Mill Grove Farm stood high on the rough banks of Perkiomen Creek, and just below the house the creek waters tumbled into the Schuylkill River. Now, in springtime, the neatly planted orchard trees were all in bloom. There were fluffy clouds of cherry and plum blossom, pale pink apple bloom, and the deeper rose blossom of peach trees.

The house was built of red stone, and it reminded him just a little of his beloved Wheatstacks. When he stood by the front door, he could look down over the swift tumbling waters of the Perkiomen Creek, across the rich bottom lands of the valley, and beyond to the dim Reading hills.

Halfway down the slope stood a stone mill, almost hidden by walnut trees, its great wheel turning slowly in the stream. The old miller was just opening the door of the mill when John went past, and he answered the boy's friendly greeting with a kindly smile.

"You're the young French lad, I reckon?" he said. "I was expecting you. Squire Thomas told me you were coming. Are you always about so early of a morning?"

"Oh, yes, morning's the best time to find the birds. I suppose there are multitudes of birds about here?"

"Not so many as'll come later. There's still snow on the hills and the wind is piercing cold. I did spy a kingfisher yesterday—spring's close when you see the kingfishers."

"And the swallows—have they come yet from the south?" the boy asked.

The old man smiled kindly at Jean. "I reckon you mean have the swallows come up from under the water yet? Everyone knows that they sleep all winter under the water and won't peep even a head out until the weather gets warm."

This made John smile to himself. He knew better than that, but he was too polite to contradict his new friend.

Then the old miller pointed up above the milldam where the mouth of a little cave made a dark spot against the high river bank.

"In yon cave are the pewees' nests. The pewees are not there yet, but they'll be back soon, now that the kingfisher's out again."

John sped up the creek to the cave. There, in the arched entrance of the stone cave, he saw a nest, made of mud and velvety moss.

"This will be my study!" thought the boy in delight. "Here I shall bring my books and pencils and paper. I shall be here to welcome the pewees when they come home. Here I shall store the rare things I find."

He burst into the kitchen of Mill Grove looking wildly happy.

"Truly the United States is a land of richness!" he cried to Mrs. Thomas, busy at the big brick oven. "Look at the treasure I have found in one little promenade!"

He began to pull things from his pockets and pile them on the spotless kitchen table—three little snakes, still sluggish from the cold weather, a handful of moss, a brightly colored feather dropped from a bird's wing, a left-over hummingbird's nest, a spray of bright red berries from a wild-rose bush.

"You call that treasure?" cried the housewife, shrinking in horror from the snakes. "I call 'em varmints!"

Mrs. Thomas was not really angry, for she had taken a quick liking to this friendly boy with the bright, attractive eyes and funny foreign way of speaking.

"You're an odd lad," she said, smiling and shaking her head. "But clear away that mess so that I can set you out some breakfast. I want you to be happy here!"

"There is no doubt of that!" cried John, carefully putting his riches onto a pewter tray. He ran up the stairs to his room, singing at the top of his voice.

"Sing, nightingale, sing on,

Joy from your glad heart bringing!"

John was certain that he had never been happier. Mr. and Mrs. Thomas were very kind, and Mill Grove seemed like a paradise to him. In many ways, it was nicer than Wheatstacks. There were countless birds, flowers, trees, and animals on the big estate, and every one was a new discovery to the eager boy.

All day long he was free to roam the fields, to ride horseback, or to wander in the deep woods. No one ever complained because he was "wasting time." There were no dull mathematics problems to study. His time was his own.

He spent hours in the cave, watching the pewees. He saw how carefully they repaired their old nests, getting ready for the summer. He caught several of them and tied tiny silver threads about their legs. "Next spring I'll look for you," he said. "I will see if you can find your way back to the Perkiomen."

❖

"There's a new family in the house at Fatland Ford," Mr. Thomas had told John. "An Englishman whose name is William Bakewell has bought the place."

"He has six children," Mrs. Thomas had added. "Most of them are girls, and very nice young ladies, I understand. Perhaps you and I should go to call on them, John."

"Heaven forbid!" John had cried. "Girls are nuisances, afraid of the snakes and without the most petite sense about birds. The English girl would be the biggest nuisance of all."

He had not yet forgotten Cecile, who had screamed in anger and fright at the sight of his lovely little snake coiled about the candle. And even Rose—had she not always complained about the smells of his room? Didn't she always say, "Jean, if you would only not get into such a frenzy over a bird!"

Even when Mr. Bakewell called at Mill Grove to invite John on a hunting trip, the boy was still stubborn. He was out on a hunting trip of his own when the new neighbor came. Mrs. Thomas took the message and told John of the invitation. "You should return the call," she said, a little concerned.

But John shook his head. "I am determined to

have nothing to do with that Bakewell family!" he declared.

Then one day some time later, when he was walking through the gold and crimson woods of autumn, he came face to face with another hunter, followed by a pair of beautiful pointer dogs.

They spent a happy morning hunting, and John admired his new friend who was skilled with his gun. He was ashamed when he learned that this was Mr. Bakewell, and he apologized for not having returned his call.

"I will visit you soon. I promise you," he said. Now he could speak English more easily.

The very next morning he knocked at the door of the stately white-pillared house of the English family, and a servant let him in.

He had put on his finest clothes and looked like a very elegant young gentleman. He wanted this family to see him at his best.

Only one person was there—a young girl who sat by the fire, sewing. She stood up to greet him. She was tall and slender, about seventeen, with gray eyes and hair the color of oak leaves in the fall.

John suddenly forgot his elegant ways and his careful English speech. But the girl did not laugh at him. She told him her father was not at home, but invited him to have a seat.

"Do you like birds?" he asked.

"My name is Lucy," she said with a pleasant friendliness.

John sat down by the fire. His shyness went away, and soon he was talking to Lucy as though he had known her for a long time.

"Do you like birds?" he asked.

Lucy replied, "Very much. Do you?"

"I adore them. They are my greatest passion," declared John. He looked at the girl's sweet face and decided that he would tell her something very important.

"I have a study in one of the caves along the

Perkiomen. I am learning about the North American birds. I am going to make pictures of them. I am going to make a picture of every American bird known to man!"

He waited to see what she would do. She did not laugh. She did not look disgusted. She did not shake her head. She smiled a little, and her eyes were wide and friendly.

"I think that would be a wonderful thing to do!" she said, earnestly.

John, happy as a lark, repeated his promise. "It will take a long time. It may take many, many, years. But I will draw them all—every bird in North America!"

What Happened Next?

• John and Lucy married and had two sons, Victor and John Woodhouse. John Woodhouse studied art and contributed to his father's life work, Birds of America. He also collaborated with his father to produce a book of animal drawings entitled The Viviparous Quadrupeds of North America. (What do viviparous and quadruped mean? See What Does That Mean to find out.)

• John James Audubon pursued his dream of making a book of life-sized pictures of the birds of North America. He traveled all over America, collecting birds, drawing pictures, and making studies.

• In 1826, John traveled to England to find a publisher for his book, Birds of America. The first volume of the Birds of America appeared in 1827 and the last came out in 1838.

• Founded in 1905 to protect our natural environment, the National Audubon Society was named for John James Audubon, artist, naturalist and explorer.

• To learn more about the National Audubon Society write:

National Audubon Society
700 Broadway
New York, New York, 10003
Or visit the website at www.audubon.org

Fun Facts about John Audubon

• John Audubon was born Jean Jacques Fougère Audubon. He changed his name to John James Audubon when he traveled to America at the age of 18.

• *Birds of America* was published as a series of 435 prints of 497 species of birds. The first print in the book is the turkey vulture and the last print is the American dipper. The original book measured 2 by 3 feet.

• John Audubon was the first known user of "bird-banding." He tied strings around the leg of a bird for identification and learned that it returned to the same nesting place each season.

• Born a French citizen, Audubon became a citizen of the United States when he was 21.

• John Audubon came to Pennsylvania to live on his father's farm, Mill Grove, in 1803. Mill Grove still exists today and is open to the public.

• Early in Audubon's career, he left drawings of nearly 1000 birds stored in a wooden box. Upon opening the box later, he discovered only bits of paper--rats had destroyed every one.

• The Audubon Museum, located in John James Audubon State Park in Henderson, KY, has the largest display of Audubon works and memorabilia in the United States.

When John Audubon Lived

Date	Event
1785	John Audubon was born in Haiti. There were 13 American states.
1803	John Audubon came to Pennsylvania and settled at Mill Grove. The United States bought the Louisiana Territory.
1807–1820	Audubon attempted several business ventures but was unsuccessful. The War of 1812 was fought, 1812-1815.
1827–1838	Audubon published his book, *Birds of America*, and lived in England. Samuel Morse invented the telegraph in 1835.
1839	Audubon returned to the United States. John D. Rockefeller was born.
1851	John Audubon died on January 27. Millard Fillmore was President of the United States.

For more information and further reading about
John Audubon, visit the **Young Patriots Series** website at
www.patriapress.com

What Does That Mean?

trogon—brightly colored forest bird that lives in warm climates.

chaff—husks separated from grain

cupola—small tower on a roof

petite—French word meaning "small"

pinions—wings of a bird

lute—a musical instrument with strings

plumage—bird's coat of feathers

spinet—a small, early form of the piano

taxidermist—person who stuffs the skins of animals to make them look lifelike.

russet—reddish brown

viviparous—producing living young that develop inside the body

quadruped—an animal with four feet used for walking

About the Author

Miriam E. Mason was born and grew up in Goshen, Indiana. In the course of her long career, she wrote more than fifty books for young readers as well as serving as an elementary school textbook consultant. Before her death in 1971, she was recognized as an Indiana Author of the Year. Her many titles written for the original *Childhood of Famous Americans Series*®, from which the **Young Patriots Series** is derived, included *Dan Beard, Mary Mapes Dodge, Kate Douglas Wiggin,* and *William Penn.*

Books in the Young Patriots Series

Volume 1 *Amelia Earhart, Young Air Pioneer*
by Jane Moore Howe

Volume 2 *William Henry Harrison,
Young Tippecanoe* by Howard Peckham

Volume 3 *Lew Wallace, Boy Writer*
by Martha E. Schaaf

Volume 4 *Juliette Low, Girl Scout Founder*
by Helen Boyd Higgins

Volume 5 *James Whitcomb Riley, Young Poet*
by Minnie Belle Mitchell and Montrew Dunham

Volume 6 *Eddie Rickenbacker, Boy Pilot and Racer*
by Kathryn Cleven Sisson

Volume 7 *Mahalia Jackson, Gospel Singer
and Civil Rights Champion* by Montrew Dunham

Volume 8 *George Rogers Clark, Boy of the
Northwest Frontier* by Katharine E. Wilkie

Volume 9 *John Hancock, Independent Boy*
by Kathryn Cleven Sisson

Volume 10 *Phillis Wheatley, Young
Revolutionary Poet*
by Kathryn Kilby Borland and Helen Ross Speicher

Volume 11 *Abner Doubleday, Boy Baseball Pioneer*
by Montrew Dunham

Volume 12 *John Audubon, Young Naturalist*
by Miriam E. Mason

Watch for more **Young Patriots** Coming Soon
Visit www.patriapress.com for updates!